MAX E. JAMES

BEACH BOUND

J. RYAN HERSEY

Illustrated by Gustavo Mazali

TABLE OF CONTENTS

To my family – the source of my inspiration.

FREE DOWNLOAD

Will Max's one and only birthday wish come true?

Join my Kids' Club to get your free copy of the second book in the Max E. James children's series.
Type the link below into your browser to get started.
http://eepurl.com/cfcfkj

CHAPTER 1

Waiting

"OH MAN," I said. "Trapped in my room. Again." It was pitch black except for the glowing red light from my desk. The numbers on the clock read five-four-three.

How could I, Max E. James, be stuck in my room? One of my parents' rules, that's how. The rule says I can't come out until the first number on the clock reads six. Thanks, Mom and Dad.

I stared at my clock for what seemed like an hour, but the numbers didn't change. Must be broken.

"That's it," I said. "Rules don't count if the clock's broken."

I grabbed Fuzzy, my best attack blanket, and tip-toed to my bedroom door for a peek down the hall. No sign of life from my big brother Cody's room. Hmm, it was a little too quiet. I remembered that Cody told me once that monsters hide in dark silent halls. Fuzzy eats monsters.

"Go get 'em!" I shouted, launching Fuzzy into the hall.

I slammed the door shut, pressed my back against it, and counted slowly.

"One...two...three...four...five," I said. "That should just about do it. Any monsters left, Fuzzy?"

I cracked the door. No trace of any beasts.

"I can always count on you," I said. "I hope they tasted good."

I grabbed Fuzzy and crept into the living room to watch cartoons.

"Would you look at that?! The clock on the TV says five-four-three, too!" I exclaimed. "What are the chances?"

I wrapped Fuzzy around me and left a small peeky hole for just my face. I felt the couch bounce as I flipped through the channels. It was Cody. He plopped down next to me and before I got a word out, he snatched the remote.

"Hey, no fair," I said. "My turn to pick."

He glared at me and turned back to the TV. I didn't stand a chance.

"That's what I thought," he said. He yanked Fuzzy away and bundled him around his feet!

"Gross," I said. "Get your dirty piggies off my blanket!"

Cody just smiled and dug his toes in deeper. I clenched my teeth, reached for the closest pillow, and swung it at his big fat head.

Faah-whap! The force sent him sailing off the couch onto the floor. The remote crashed down beside him.

"Serves you right," I said.

"You'll pay for that," he said, wobbling to his feet.

I slid off the couch and backed away.

"Ahhh! Mom-my!" I cried. "He's going to get me!"

I raced towards my room and heard a thud behind me. What was that? I turned around and slammed into Daddy, then fell backwards onto the floor. When I looked up, I saw that he was wearing a frown.

"Oh. Hello, Daddy," I said. "It's still early. What are you doing up?"

"What's going on, Max?" he asked. "It sounds like a herd of elephants out here."

"No pachyderms," I said. "It's just—"

"He hit me in the face!" Cody said. "And made me fall, too."

"No, I didn't," I said. "It's not my fault you can't walk."

"Is everybody okay?" Daddy asked.

"Yup," I said.

"I guess so, but my butt hurts," Cody said.

Daddy knelt down, rubbing his forehead. "Let me see."

Cody pointed to a red blotch just below his hip.

"Mommy said not to rub your head like that,"

I said. "Remember? It will give you a retreating hairline."

Just then, Mommy walked out of their room, giggling.

"Good morning, gentlemen," she said. "By the way, Max, that's a *receding* hairline. But you're right, Daddy's hair is retreating." She kissed us each on the cheek and walked down the hall.

"Oh, and, Daddy," she said, "it's only 5:50. Should they be out of their rooms this early?"

Daddy smiled at Cody and me. He leaned close. "You boys know the rules. Back to your rooms."

So there I was, right where I started. Trapped. The worst part? I didn't even find out what we were going to do today. I looked at my clock. It said five-five-one.

CHAPTER 2

Mommy's Pearly Whites

"THANK YOU, SIX." I said. "I'm free at last." I ran to the kitchen and was greeted by the smell of bacon and pancakes. My favorite!

"Well, good morning, again," Mommy said. "Please wash your hands before you sit down."

"What?" I said. "But I haven't even touched anything dirty today. They're clean, see?"

I stretched my hands into the air and wiggled my fingers inches from her face.

"Go wash your hands," Mommy said, laughing.

I washed them as fast as I could and was back to the table in a flash.

"Yummy," I said. "I love the smell of bacon."

"And the taste, too," Cody said.

My first bite was almost spoiled by a horrible smell: Daddy's coffee.

"Yuck, Daddy," I said. "Your liquid stink is ruining my taste adventure."

He must have choked on that nasty stuff because he spit some out all over the table. Coffee must taste as bad as it smells.

I leaned close to him and smiled. He smiled back. Now's my chance! I jammed my fingers into his mouth and yanked on his two front teeth.

"Ouch!" he said. "What in the world are you doing?"

"Well, you drink coffee."

"Uh-huh."

"So I wanted to see how easily your teeth came out. They're really stuck in there good."

"What are you talking about, Max?" Mommy asked.

Cody stopped chewing and stared at me.

"What?" I said. "I saw it on TV. Old people take their teeth out to clean off coffee stains. They put them in cups of bubbly water."

Cody rolled his eyes. "Those are dentures, genius. You know, fake teeth."

"Oh, I forgot," I said. "You're nine now so you know everything."

"Dentures are for really old people who don't have their real teeth anymore," Cody said. "You have to be like thirty or forty to get them."

Unfortunately, the roar of laughter from Mommy and Daddy saved Cody from getting in trouble for making fun of me.

"One thing's for sure," Daddy said. "That boy is getting too much screen time."

Cody looked up at Mommy's bright red face. "How old are you?"

"I'm thirty-nine, Cody," Mommy said.

"Oh," he said.

Now Mr. Smarty-pants didn't know if their teeth were real or not.

Mommy revealed all of her pearly whites with a warm smile. "Don't worry. All my teeth are real. And so are Daddy's."

We finished breakfast and I ran to my room. A t-shirt and my favorite swimming trunks had been laid out on my bed.

"Mom-my! Are we going swimming?"

"We're going to the beach, Max," she said. "But not quite yet. I still have to take a shower."

My face crumbled. "But I already had to wait once today. I can't wait anymore."

"Well, you're going to have to," Mommy said.

"Ugh," I mumbled. Time stands still when mommies are in the bathroom.

"Why don't you go help load the truck?" she said. "I think your Daddy and Cody are already outside."

As I stepped onto the driveway, the sun warmed my cheeks.

"Grab those bodyboards, Max," Daddy said.

I felt uneasy as I reached for the boards, but I couldn't put my finger on why. Their salty smell snapped me out of my trance. Oh well, I thought, and handed them to Daddy.

After everything was packed, Cody and I hopped in the back seat and buckled up.

Daddy stood outside the truck shaking his head. As he opened the door, he said, "Gentlemen, it's not time to go yet. Out of the truck."

"Can't we just wait in here?" Cody asked.

"We're so excited," I said.

"Fine, but crack the windows so you can breathe."

Cody and I smiled at each other and rolled the windows down.

"And no fighting!" He pointed his finger at us and ducked into the house.

"Yeah," Cody said. He flicked my ear. "No fighting, Max. Stay on your side!"

"Ouch!" I said. "Keep it up and we won't even make it out of the driveway."

I laid a towel across the back seat to separate our sides.

"There," I said. "Don't you dare cross it."

CHAPTER 3

Sand in My Toes

KNOCK-KNOCK. THE RAP on the window startled me.

"You're both still breathing," Mommy said as she got into the truck. "No blood even. I'm impressed."

Daddy sat down in the driver's seat and we were off.

"What do you want to do now?" I asked. "Car rides are boring."

"I don't know," Cody said. "How about a thumb wrestling tournament?"

"Sounds good to me. No cheating though, okay?"

He smiled and we interlocked hands to kick off the first match.

"One-two-three-four!" we chanted. "I declare a thumb war."

Even though Cody's older, we're pretty evenly matched when it comes to thumb wrestling. I won the first bout, then he won the second. By the time we turned onto the beach road, the score was tied at seven to seven.

"Look!" I said. "I see water."

"We're almost there," Cody said. "Last match."

He looked me dead in the eye. "This one is for all the glory."

I lunged at his thumb, but it slipped out from under my grip. That's when he extended his pointer finger and snagged my thumb. I was down for the count.

"One. Two. Three! Please welcome the all-time reigning thumb-wrestling champion of the world!" shouted Cody.

"Hey," I said. "You cheated! The Japanese Snake Attack is illegal."

"Too bad, little brother," he said. "There's always next time."

The truck ground to a halt and he wiggled his finger in my face and hissed like a snake. "We're at the beach now anyway. The tournament is over."

We cleared the parking lot and hit the sand. Cody and I sped off with our bodyboards. Mommy

followed with the towels and her purse. Daddy car-
ried everything else.

Cody and I ran onto the trail past the sign at the
base of the dunes. It said: No Walking on Dunes.

Thanks to my run-in with the park ranger last
summer, I know that the sign means no climbing
either. Or jumping and rolling. I suggested they
needed a bigger sign listing all the rules. Apparently

there is some kind of nature living there, but all I've ever seen is grass and weeds.

"Do you hear that, Max?" Cody asked.

I stopped to listen.

"Is that the waves?" I asked.

"Oh man. If you can hear them from here, they're going to be huge!"

Cody zoomed down the path out of sight.

My stomach twisted and turned as memories of last summer flooded my mind. Oh, right! I know why the bodyboards made me feel funny. The last time I bodyboarded, I face-planted in the sand after a huge wave spit me up on the beach. It was horrible! I sure hope it doesn't happen again!

Since Cody had ditched me, I walked the rest of the way with Mommy and Daddy. As we were setting up I remembered the one thing I can't stand about the beach.

"I hate sunscreen!" I yelled. "It makes the sand stick to me and Daddy gets it in my eyes. It burns."

"Well, it's either that or spend the day in the truck," Daddy said. "Your choice."

"Wait a minute."

I rummaged through the sand toys and pulled out a pair of goggles.

"There," I said, adjusting the strap and sliding them over my head. "Ready."

Daddy chuckled and rubbed the sticky goo all over me.

"Sorry, buddy," he said. "You know I have to."

Cody grabbed his bodyboard and headed to the water after Mommy finished with his sunscreen. Something caught my eye as he sprinted past.

There's only one type of nature that moves like that, I thought.

"Hurry up, Daddy," I said. "Before it escapes!"

"Before what escapes?" he asked.

"That nature over there. It's the best kind— alive!"

CHAPTER 4

Unsuspecting Nature

"COME ON, DADDY," I said. "This is taking forever."

"All done," he said.

I grabbed my net and took off. When I got to the spot where I'd seen the movement, I dropped down and crept across the warm sand. Bad move. I was instantly coated from head to toe. Human sand paper once again. Thanks a lot, Daddy.

I crawled over a mound and removed my goggles. Inches from my nose lay a perfectly round hole the size of my fist. Jack pot! It was a ghost crab lair. I peered down the dark the tunnel.

"Anyone home?" I whispered.

Nothing. There was no way I was going to stick my hand in there. I learned that lesson the hard way last summer! Instead, I jammed the net handle down the hole and it disappeared beneath the sand.

"How about now?" I said.

I wiggled the handle in circles, causing a partial tunnel collapse.

"I guess I'll have to wait you out," I said.

"Hey!" a voice called from behind me. "What are you doing?"

"Shhhhh, I found a ghost crab," I said. "He's down this hole. I'm going to catch him."

"Here, let me help you," Cody said. "He won't come if you're too close."

I shrugged my shoulders.

"You have to move farther back."

"But my net is too short. How will I reach?"

"We could build a trap!" Cody said.

"How?"

"Like you see in the cartoons. All we need is a bucket, some string, and a stick. Works every time, guaranteed."

"I don't have any string," I said.

"Go ask Mommy and Daddy. I'll keep watch while you're gone."

I took off through the sand. Turns out Daddy had some old fishing line at the bottom of the beach bag. That line would work just fine for our trap.

"Thanks," I said.

I grabbed Cody's net and stuffed the fishing line in the bucket. Now I just needed a stick.

I searched the beach but didn't even find a twig.

"Hmm," I said, wondering what else could work. "I know. I've got it!"

I pulled an old army man from the toy bag.

"Duty calls," I said and ran back to find Cody still standing guard. I dropped the supplies on the ground in front of him.

"Looks like you got everything but the stick, Max."

"I couldn't find one," I said. "Anyway, this is better."

I held the old army man close to his face.

"Meet Sergeant Crab Trap."

"What's he for?" Cody asked.

"His mission is to hold up the bucket! Sergeant Crab Trap reporting for duty, Sir!" I said in my best army man voice.

Cody smiled. "Interesting idea."

I put the bucket down beside the tunnel and waited while Cody tied the fishing line around the sergeant.

"Here you go," Cody said, and he threw it to me.

I stuck Sergeant Crab Trap in the sand next to the hole. I leaned the bucket against his shoulder, making sure to keep his view clear.

"Careful with the fishing line," I said.

Cody gently laid it across the sand. "Now, we wait."

We huddled behind a mound of sand, but didn't have to wait long before we saw something more. I tightened my grip on the line.

"Look," I said. "There it is!"

A single leg emerged. Then there were two legs but they vanished in a white flash.

"Did you see that?" I said.

"Yup. Won't be long—,"

"Look!"

Two beady black eyes popped out of the hole. They were followed by legs and a claw. He was almost completely out.

"Get ready," I said. "Just a little farther."

We held our breath in silence. My sweaty hands grasped the line even tighter.

The white crab surfaced and cautiously searched the area.

"He doesn't look so fast," I said.

"Trust me," said Cody. "He's like lightning. Pull on three?"

I nodded.

"One. Two. Three!"

I yanked the line as hard as I could. Sergeant Crab Trap skipped across the beach and the bucket clipped the crab as it fell. It scurried across the sand towards us.

"Hey," I said. "It missed. The trap is a dud."

"Have faith, little brother," Cody said.

He pointed at the bucket. It came to rest directly over the tunnel.

"We got him now!" he said. "Get him."

The crab darted across the beach frantically searching for a place to hide. Cody lunged in front of him and I snuck around behind.

"Net him, Max."

We both swiped our nets, but he scampered away. Cody threw his net as the crab ran past. He missed, but the stunned crab paused just long enough for me to scoop him up from behind.

"Yes!" I cried. "I got him."

"All right," Cody said. "I knew we could do it."

I held the net up and admired our catch. He was the size of my fist.

"Get the bucket, Max! Before he escapes."

We ran back to our stuff and grabbed the bucket. Cody filled it halfway with sand and dumped the crab in.

"Look, Mommy," I said, running toward her. "We caught a ghost crab."

It circled the bucket, trying to jump out, but the walls were too high.

"I think I will name him Hobart," I said.

"Very nice, gentlemen," Mommy said. "Please

don't leave him in there all day. He's happier when he's free."

Mommy pulled down her glasses so we could see her eyes. "Okay?"

"You mean we can't keep him?" I said. "He's our pet."

"No, Max. He has to go back to the wild before we leave."

"Okay," I said. "Whew! All that work made me sweaty. It's dripping all down my face."

"Time to get back in the water," Cody said.

He turned and raced to the ocean. I ran after him, but paused at Mommy's feet.

"Don't let him escape."

"I'll keep an eye on him," she said. "But if he gets out, I'm not touching him."

Chapter 5

Cannonball Wave

I CHASED AFTER Cody only to grind to a halt steps later. A drop of sweaty sunscreen trickled into my eyes.

"Ow! It burns!" I yelled.

Rubbing it just spread the liquid fire. I stumbled to the water's edge in a blind daze. If only I could rinse it out. I bent down and splashed some water on my face.

"Ahh!"

The salt water burned even more. I blinked uncontrollably and collapsed in misery. Tears filled my eyes. Drop by drop, they flushed the pain away.

My vision was blurry, but I could just make out a figure in the water: Cody.

"Wait for me," I said.

I waded carefully into the water as Cody dove

into a wave up ahead. My toes dug into the sand with each light step. Careful now. I didn't want to land on any sharp or pinchy nature. Cut feet end the day real quick.

Just then, I stepped on something soft and slippery. It was slimy and wiggled under my foot.

"Gross," I said. "Co-dy. I stepped on a big...a big, booger! And it's moving."

It flipped and flopped real mad. I lifted my foot and just like that, it was gone. At least it didn't pinch me.

I swam all the way to Cody without my feet touching the bottom. I clutched his waist and lifted my feet to his face.

"Do you see any slime?" I wiggled my toes. "Any booger pieces?"

"Are you all right?" Cody asked.

I nodded my head, so Cody pried me off and I dropped into the water.

"Don't worry. It was probably just a flounder. They lie flat on the bottom."

"Oh," I said. "Do they bite?"

"No, but they're weird. Their eyes are only on one side of their head."

"Who's eyes?" asked Daddy.

He sloshed through the water towards us.

"The flounder Max just stepped on," Cody said.

"Oh," Daddy said. "I bet that was freaky. What are you guys doing out here?"

"Getting ready for our favorite beach game," Cody said. "That is if you say yes."

"What?" Daddy said.

"Cannonball wave!" we shouted.

"Aren't you guys getting a little too big to stand on my shoulders?"

"Nope," Cody said.

"Me neither," I said.

Daddy rubbed his shoulders and stretched his arms.

"Okay, but no diving."

"Me first," I said. I swam over and scurried up his back.

"Easy now," Daddy said as I climbed onto his shoulders.

"Jump already!" Cody said.

I leapt and the oncoming wave swallowed me with a splash.

"Nice one," Daddy said. "The waves are perfect today, huh boys?"

Cody climbed onto Daddy's shoulders as I swam back towards them.

"Sure are," Cody said. "It's going to be great for bodyboarding."

"Yeah," I said softly. "But not right now, okay? More cannonballs."

We took turns jumping into the oncoming waves. As I scaled him for what must have been the fifteenth time, something caught my eye.

"What's that?" I asked.

Daddy and Cody turned to look. I pointed to the little splashes peppering the top of the water.

"Probably little fish," Daddy said. "Why do you suppose they're jumping?"

"To breathe?" I said.

"No," Cody said. "They're lunch for something bigger."

"Cody's right," Daddy said. "Fish breathe underwater. Something is definitely chasing them."

"Look!" Cody said. "Behind you!"

I turned in time to see a large dark fin slice through the water only feet from us.

CHAPTER 6

Digging Like a Ghost Crab

I SCRAMBLED UP Daddy's back and clung to his neck with white knuckles.

"What was that?!" I asked, frantic.

"Neck. Loosen," he croaked.

I eased my death grip.

"Look over there," Cody said. He pointed at three gray fins that disappeared in a swirl of baitfish.

"Those look like shark fins," I said softly.

"I bet they're dolphin," said Cody.

"That's a pod of dolphin," Daddy said. "Must be lunchtime. We sure are lucky to see them up close in the wild."

"Yay," I said. "Unsuspecting wild nature."

Every time one surfaced, I felt an urge to swim

with them. I closed my eyes and imagined gliding through the water holding onto a fin. Now's my only chance, I thought.

I sprang off Daddy's shoulders and paddled furiously towards the pod of dolphin. I was almost within reach when I felt a tug on my foot. I kicked and tried to jerk free, but it was no use. I gave up the struggle and turned to find Daddy holding my foot.

"Excuse me," I said. "I can't reach the dolphin with you holding me. Please let go."

"Exactly," Daddy said. "They're wild animals eating lunch. We should keep our distance."

"But I want to swim with them and teach them tricks," I said. "Does anyone have a hoop?"

"I think it's time for a break from the water," Daddy said. "Let's go play on the beach."

"But I want to stay here," I said.

"Come on, Max," he said. "We can dig a hole."

"A deep one?"

"We'll see."

We all sloshed through the water back to shore where Mommy was sunbathing.

"Looked like fun out there," she said. "Did you see the dolphin?"

"Sure did," I said. "I was going to train them, but Daddy wouldn't let me."

"Didn't even come close," Cody said. "I'm going skim boarding." He grabbed his board and was off.

I rummaged through the bag of sand toys and pulled out two shovels.

"This one's for you," I said. I motioned for Daddy to take the shovel.

Mommy giggled.

"A father's work is never done," she said.

"Okay, Max. I'll help, but I'm not going to dig it for you."

"Let's make it deep."

"Oh no," Mommy said, "No bottomless pit this time. Someone almost fell into one of your holes last summer, remember?"

"Yes," I said. "And I would have caught that man too. But you had to go and warn him."

Mommy slowly rubbed the sides of her head and glared at Daddy.

"Reasonable depth, Daddy."

I frowned at him. Just great. A reasonable depth is like those mini chocolate bars, never enough.

"Sure thing," Daddy said.

He winked at me and I smiled back, because he's just a big kid that looks like an adult. I bet he likes digging holes more than I do. It goes much faster when he helps, too. He does most of the work while I watch. He thinks I'm going to make a good manager someday— whatever that means.

"Try that," he said.

I jumped into the hole. "Not deep enough yet." I climbed out of the hole and waited patiently for him to finish.

"How about now?"

I jumped in and started scooping out buckets of sand.

"I think that's reasonable," he said. "I don't want to get in trouble with Mom."

I slid down the side and disappeared into the cool sand. I popped my head up and peeked over the edge. Daddy laughed.

"You remind me of a ghost crab," he said.

"Ghost crab?" I said. I'd forgotten all about my new pet. "Hobart! I'm coming!"

I scrambled out of the hole and raced to Mommy.

When I looked into the bucket where I'd left Hobart, all I saw was sand. "Mommy, where's Hobart?" I asked. "Didn't you watch him?"

She sat up from sunbathing and took off her sunglasses. "He's not in the bucket?" she asked. "I'm sorry, Honey. He must have escaped."

"I wonder how he got out."

I studied the bucket. There weren't any tracks or tunnels. The sand was totally smooth.

"He must have jumped out," I said and stuffed my hand deep into the bucketful of sand where he'd been.

CHAPTER 7

Hobart's Revenge

I ROOTED AROUND and discovered something hard under the cool sand. "What's that?" I didn't remember putting a rock in there. Could it be? The hard thing wiggled and I froze.

Snap!

"Ahh!" I jerked my hand out and there was Hobart, dangling from my throbbing finger. The sharp pain surged up my arm.

"Let go!" I said and whipped my hand back and forth. The crab sailed through the air and skipped across the beach. He settled a few feet from me and wobbled about.

"Bad Hobart." I shook my tender finger at him. "Pets aren't supposed to pinch."

The ghost crab retreated through the sand and

was quickly out of sight. He didn't even look sorry for what he'd done.

I turned to my parents.

"Can you believe it?" I said. "He pinched me!"

I shoved my finger close to their faces.

"See," I said. "Right there." I pointed to the broken skin at the tip.

Mommy let out a snort and covered her mouth.

Daddy turned away. I think he was trying to avoid looking at me.

"Are you kidding? This is serious! I almost lost a finger," I said, stepping closer. "And you think it's funny?"

Daddy erupted with laughter. Mommy managed to contain all but a few soft giggles.

"I'm sorry, Max," she said. "What did you expect? Are you okay?"

"I'm all right, but Hobart had to leave on account of his bad attitude."

"I guess he turned out not to be such a good pet?" she said.

"No, he wasn't." I turned back in the direction he'd fled, then felt my stomach grumble.

"Was that you?" she asked.

"I haven't eaten since breakfast," I said. "I think I need a snack."

"It is about time for lunch," Mommy said. "Cody! Time to eat."

Cody ran up, spotted the empty bucket, and shook his head.

"It was an accident," I said. "He pinched me."

"How?"

"I thought he escaped, so I dug him up."

Cody laughed. "Serves you right. You know ghost crabs burrow in the sand."

"Yeah," I said. "But I didn't think my very own pet would pinch me."

"Okay," Mommy said. "Sit down and I'll pass out the peanut butter and jelly sandwiches. We also have watermelon and chips. Please don't get sand in your food—crunchy sandwiches are gross."

"But I like crunchy peanut butter," Cody said.

Mommy squinted sharply at us, so we stopped giggling and ate.

I devoured my watermelon. It was cool and sweet in the hot summer sun.

I crunched my chips and bit into my sandwich. That's when I remembered another one of my parents' favorite rules: no swimming after you eat. They make you wait fifteen minutes before getting back in the water after eating. I kicked Cody and he looked up at me.

"Tricked again," I said.

"What are you talking about?" he asked.

"We have to wait fifteen whole minutes before we get back in the water!"

I stood and chucked the rest of my sandwich down the beach. Mommy did not miss this little act.

"Pick it up!" she snapped.

I slouched slowly towards the crust of bread.

Keow! Keow! Keow!

"What was tha—"

A lone seagull dove past my head as it swooped in and snatched up the sandy treat.

I turned back to Cody who was sprinting towards me.

"Try a chip next," he said.

"No, Max," Daddy said. "Don't throw anything."

I grabbed a handful of chips and tossed them in

the air. In an instant, a cloud of seagulls was upon us. They inhaled the offering and hovered just out of reach, hoping for more.

"One at a time now," I said. "I'm almost out."

Cody and I took turns throwing chips. The seagulls squawked and competed as they dive-bombed the crumbs.

Daddy took a step toward us. I could see his red face glistening in the sun.

"Let them be," Mommy said. She grasped his arm. "You've already warned them."

"Warned us?" Cody said. "What are they talking about?"

Splat!

I closed my eyes and felt sick to my stomach. The warm goo slid down my shoulder onto my arm. The chips I had just eaten soured in my belly. I swallowed hard against the knot in my throat.

"Eww!" Cody said. "Direct hit."

I opened my eyes to see the white sludge and gagged.

"Get it off!"

"I'm not touching that," he said and slinked backwards, but not far enough to escape his own poop shower.

Splat!

A large dropping landed right on Cody's foot.

"Yuck!" he said, kicking hard to fling most of it off.

We dropped the rest of our food and ran to Mommy and Daddy.

I expected a lecture, but they burst into laughter at the sight of us.

"Don't look at me," Daddy said between chuckles. Go wash off in the water."

"Maybe next time you'll listen to us," Mommy said.

Cody and I ran to the shore to wash off the poop.

"Use some sand to scrub so you don't have to touch it," Cody said. It seemed to do the trick.

Daddy appeared behind us in the surf. "Thirty-minute warning, boys. We have to leave soon, so it's now or never if we're going to go bodyboarding."

Before I could utter a word, he was towing us out into the waves. Suddenly, I wondered what had happened to the fifteen-minute rule.

CHAPTER 8

Time to Come Clean

DADDY TRUDGED THROUGH the water. The boards slapped the waves after he hauled us over each whitecap. Somehow we managed to hang on.

"Whew," I said. "We sure are a long way from shore."

"Okay," Daddy said. "Let me know when you see a good one."

I wiped the hair from my eyes and stared at the horizon. The butterflies in my stomach seemed to keep time with the swell.

"Be sure to paddle when I push," he said. "Soon you'll be doing this on your own."

"I want to go first!" Cody said.

"Fine with me," I said. "I think I'll just wait a bit. You know, for the perfect wave."

"I see one," Cody said. He pointed behind us. "Quick, turn me around."

"Hang tight here, Max," Daddy said.

I bobbed over the steep wave and watched him guide Cody into position.

"Now paddle," he said.

Cody thrashed though the water as the surf swept him away.

I looked up at Daddy and tried to swallow.

"Did he make it?"

Daddy shrugged his shoulders and smiled.

I heard a faint call from the beach.

"Ya-hoo!"

It was Cody. He had washed up on shore and was still on the bodyboard!

"Okay, Max. You're next."

"I'm not ready yet," I said. "Can we wait a few minutes?"

"Sure, buddy," he said. "Is something wrong?"

"No, just looking for a bigger wave," I said.

A flash of heat rushed through my body and settled in my rosy cheeks. What I really wanted was a tiny wave, and deep down I knew it.

"Are you sure you want to do this, Max?"

"Well, the truth is I've been scared ever since last summer."

"I see," he said.

Cody paddled up with a huge grin on his face. "That was awesome. I want to go again!"

Daddy smiled at me. "See, it was awesome."

"Let him take the next one then," I said. "I'm still waiting for the perfect wave."

Daddy shoved Cody onto another wave while I floated like a nervous cork waiting to finish our chat. How could I get out of this without being crunched by a wave?

"Okay," he said. "Learning something new is hard and you have to work at it. Failing can hurt, but that's how we learn."

He leaned down and put both hands on my shoulders. "You can only succeed after you fail. Got it?"

"Yeah," I said. "I get that waves can cram sand in all your cracks and crevices even with a bathing suit on."

"That's true," he said. "But it's normal to crash."

"My feet went over my head, Daddy. I had to pick sand out of my teeth for days. You call that normal?"

"No. But that wasn't a normal wipeout. You'll do better today."

I looked down at the water and shuffled my feet in the sand.

"You can swim, right?"

I nodded.

"Can hold your breath?"

"Yeah, I guess."

"Didn't we spend almost an hour jumping into breaking waves?"

"Uh-huh."

"How's that any different?"

"For starters," I said, "my face didn't get pounded into the sand. Which hurts."

"Does it hurt enough to make you not want to do this?"

"Not do what?" Cody asked as he paddled up. "Catch a wave?"

"I want to do it, but I'm scared," I said.

"There's nothing to be afraid of," Cody said. "Wiping out doesn't hurt."

I shook my head and stepped backwards.

"Easy for you to say. You don't wipeout."

"Anymore," Cody added. "I don't wipeout, any-more. When I was your age, I crashed all the time. That's how I learned."

"You did?" I said. This was news to me. It never

occurred to me that he wasn't born a good bodyboarder.

"Sure," Cody said. "But I always got back up and tried again. If everyone thought like you're thinking now, nobody would walk."

"Huh?" I said.

"How many times do you think babies fall before they get it right?"

I thought for a minute and felt a surge of courage rise within me.

"I think I'm ready now."

Cody winked at me and turned back towards the ocean.

"Great, Max," Daddy said. "Let's go catch one."

All of a sudden, Cody paddled furiously past us. "Must...get...over...it."

I turned back to see a wall of water rolling towards us.

Cody gave me a thumbs-up. "You can do it, Max." Then he drifted out of sight.

"Too late to escape it," Daddy said. "Hold on tight."

He spun me into position and gave me a shove. I felt the power as I rose from the sea. Time stopped and all was quiet in the shadow of the wave. My only thought was that I was glad no one could see the warm trail of courage leaking from my swimming trunks.

CHAPTER 9

Head Over Heels

I CLUTCHED THE board tight to my chest. My fingernails dug into the foam as I shut my eyes and sped down the steep wave. I was still gaining speed when I heard what sounded like a clap of thunder. It was the wave breaking! I knew I had to hold on a little longer. And just like that, the board slowed and my knees dug into the sand. I opened my eyes to find I had washed up on the beach and was surrounded by bubbly foam.

"I did it!" I said.

Mommy applauded from behind me. I stood in the knee-deep water and bowed to Daddy and Cody in the distance.

"How fun was that?" Mommy said.

"It was awesome. I can't wait to go again."

"I knew you could do it, Max."

"Thanks."

Cody washed up behind me and put his arm around me.

"That was a gnarly wave," he said. "You're crazy."

My chest swelled with pride and my smile stretched from ear to ear.

"Let's go again," I said and took off through the waves.

"Hey guys," Mommy said. "This is your twenty minute warning. I'll start packing while you catch a few more waves."

We ran until the water reached our waists and paddled the rest of the way out.

"We're on the clock, Daddy," Cody said pointing to the beach. "Mommy's packing up."

"Let's not waste any time then," he said. "Come on."

We spent the next twenty minutes riding wave after wave. I turned to catch another and noticed Mommy pointing to her wrist. I tapped Daddy on the shoulder and pointed.

"I'd better go help her," Daddy said. "You think you can manage the last wave without me?"

We nodded. I guess you're never too old to get in trouble with Mommy, and Daddy knew it.

"Don't worry," Cody said. "I'll help Max."

Daddy smiled and turned towards shore.

Cody and I glided over a few small waves. He bobbed beside me, holding my board close to his so I didn't slide out of reach. Luckily, we didn't have to wait long.

"That one looks good," he said and shoved me into its path.

"Wait!" I said. But it was too late. The wave scooped me up and I was headed for shore.

It didn't feel right. I rose up too fast and it

crested too soon. I started down the wave and felt the back of the board lift. The next thing I knew, I was gasping for air and tumbling toward the shore. The salt water burned as it shot up my nose. I eventually escaped from its foamy grasp and dragged my bodyboard onto the sand.

I was standing at the water's edge coughing when I felt a friendly hand on the back of my neck. It was Cody.

"Are you all right? That looked pretty nasty."

"It was," I said and spit out some sand. "But I'm okay."

Cody rubbed my sandy hair.

"Let's go before we have to walk home."

We rinsed off and changed into dry clothes before getting into the truck. I felt a cool burst of air as I opened the door. The air conditioning felt wonderful.

"I bet you boys are tired," Mommy said.

"Not hardly," I said.

"Me either," Cody said. "I want to stay longer."

"Well I am," Daddy said. He closed the door and sank into the seat. "Everyone buckled up?"

We nodded.

"Let's go," Mommy said. "Hey boys, what was your favorite part of the day?"

"Bodyboarding," Cody said. "No wait, catching Hobart. Hmm. I don't know."

"Bodyboarding, even though I was scared at first," I said and turned to Cody. "Thanks for the help."

"What are big brothers for?" Cody said.

I slumped into my seat and relaxed. But the blowing air conditioning made my eyes start to sting. I adjusted the vent and rubbed them. Must be irritated from the saltwater. I'll just rest them for a minute.

Clank!

I opened my eyes and glanced down at my shirt. There was a small puddle of drool. I wiped my chin as my door opened.

"I guess you were tired after all?" Mommy said. "You slept all the way home."

"I only closed my eyes for a minute. Wow! Time travel."

"I don't know about that," she said, "but time passes quickly when you sleep."

I scratched my chin and grinned. "That is good information."

Cody and I made our way into the house, collapsed onto the couch, and flipped on the television.

"You guys relax while we get cleaned up and ready for dinner," Daddy said.

"Dinner?" I said. "Is the day almost over?"

"I'm afraid so."

"Thank goodness for that!" I said.

Daddy looked puzzled and took a step closer. "What? Didn't you have a good time today?"

"Of course I did," I said. "How could you ask a question like that?"

"I guess I just expected a little more resistance. I didn't think you'd be happy about the day ending."

I looked at him real funny.

"Are you feeling okay?" he asked.

"Daddy," I said. "Come closer."

He leaned in. "Yes?"

"You probably don't know this, but I discovered time travel today.

"I see," he said.

"It only works when you sleep," I said. "So the sooner I get to bed, the faster I'll wake up."

"And then what?"

I smiled. "Then I can find out what we're going to do tomorrow!"

FROM THE AUTHOR

If you enjoyed this book, please leave an honest review. Word-of-mouth is truly powerful, and your words will make a huge difference. Thank you.

As you read this, I'm writing the next Max E. James adventure. For updates on new releases, promotions, and other great children's book recommendations, join my Kids' Club at:

http://www.maxejames.com/kids-club/

DON'T FORGET YOUR FREE DOWNLOAD

Type the link below into your browser to get started.
http://eepurl.com/cfcfkj

About the Author

J. Ryan Hersey is a devoted father and husband who lives in beautiful Hampton Roads, Virginia. His stories are inspired by the adventures he shares with his wife and two boys. He is author of the Max E. James children's series. To find out more or connect with him directly, visit his website at:

http://www.maxejames.com.

About the Illustrator

Gustavo Mazali lives with his family in beautiful Buenos Aires, Argentina. Having drawn all his life, Gustavo has developed the unique ability to capture the essence of children in his art. You can view his portfolio at:

http://www.mazali.com.

About the Editor

Amy Betz founded Tiny Tales Editing after working as a children's book editor at several major publishing houses. She lives with her family in Bethel, Connecticut. You can learn more about Amy at: http://www.tinytalesediting.com.

ALL TITLES

Beach Bound
Birthday Bash: Part 1
Birthday Bash: Part 2
Fishing Fever
Winter Wipeout
Crash Course

Made in the USA
Lexington, KY
29 November 2019